FROM PIMPLES TO WRINKLES

I'm Pedaling as Fast as I Can

Published by Advantage, Charleston, South Carolina.

Member of Advantage Media Group.

ADVANTAGE is a registered trademark and the Advantage colophon is a trademark of Advantage Media Group, Inc.

Printed in the United States of America

ISBN: 978-1-59932-069-4
LCCN: 2008926315

Most Advantage Media Group titles are available at special quantity discounts for bulk purchases for sales promotions, premiums, fundraising, and educational use. Special versions or book excerpts can also be created to fit specific needs.

For more information, please write: Special Markets, Advantage Media Group, P.O. Box 272, Charleston, SC 29402 or call 1.866.775.1696.

FROM PIMPLES TO WRINKLES

I'm Pedaling as Fast as I Can

Sandra J. Mullen

Advantage®

DEDICATION

I dedicate this book to my mother. She possessed an incredible gift called humor. This she passed on to me, her only daughter. This gift has served me well.

I also dedicate this book to my only daughter, Bailey. I love you with everything I am. I now pass this gift to you wrapped in the sense to use it to your life's full advantage.

A special thank you goes out to the father of my children, Michael. You have become an incredible single dad.

Great gratitude and love goes out to my wonderful Aunt "Sam" and my best gal pal Suzanne. They diligently and laboriously read and re-read this book, helping with all the corrections and changes needed to make it just right and a work I am truly proud to say is mine.

Major kudos go out to my illustrator, Amanda Russell. At twenty-two years young, she envisions beyond her years. She ran with nothing more than a concept and ultimately created a character that embodies the whimsically profound, midlife woman I had in mind. She is an incredibly talented young woman who has a very bright future. It was an honor and a pleasure to work with her on this endeavor.

I am also extremely grateful for each and every person that has come in and gone out of my life, and for the indelible marks they have placed upon it. I am the woman I am today because of all of you, my loving family, and the unconditionally loving and forgiving "man upstairs."

sjm

Prologue

LIFE'S CLOSET

Life is like a closet. After many months, sometimes years, we are forced most reluctantly to weed out many of its accumulations. Some of this paraphernalia has outlasted its useful purpose, and some we have just outgrown. I am not referring to a change in our weight. I am referring to the changes in our lives.

As we stand at the forefront, our closet doors wide open, gazing at all the stuff and not knowing where to begin, we have bestowed upon ourselves the duty—or more appropriately, the task—of determining what must stay, what must go, and what we will neatly pack away for another day. This closet, our closet, is really our personal life's space.

Parting every hanger and thoroughly examining every shelf, each piece of clothing and every memento, like the pieces of our lives, evokes a memory. Some of the apparel and tightly packed and stored boxes are glorious, labeled with laughter, warmth, and fond reflection; while others are painful, labeled with sadness, distress, and heartbreak.

Some of us are collectors, saving all the bits of our history, never letting go. We have French francs from our first trip abroad, that sexy black dress that left him breathless, and multitudes of pictures depicting our rites of passage. In the recesses of our closets, buried behind our crammed pieces of clothing and cluttered boxes of mementoes, underneath layers of dust and marked by time, you will discover our very old luggage—metaphorically, our life's baggage.

The rest of us are the "when in doubt, throw it out" types. We salvage nothing. Our motto is *out with the old, in with the new*, never giving life's memories a moment's reflection. We know all too well that if we gaze and ponder too seriously, we will become collectors. We sacrifice the laughter, warmth, and fond reflection so as to not endure the discomforts that can accompany the collector trait. If we haven't used, worn, or examined it in six months, our agenda is to dispose of it and start anew. In our closets, sitting conspicuously on the shelf is our carry-on baggage, always available at a moment's notice—for we travel light.

Which closet keeper are you? I would tend to believe, and this is only the opinion of a forty-eight year old woman who has the tendency to be more of a collector, that neither extreme is truly healthy.

Our life's closets are filled with multitudes of memories, good and bad. Some elicit beaming smiles and warm fuzzy feelings, while others bring tears and sullen remorse. It takes both to appreciate the ever-changing beauty of life. We must open the doors to let the fresh air in and weed out a few old memories in order to house the new. We gain such knowledge from our sadness and mistakes but should not linger with them too long. We can only truly appreciate the blissful memories and the glorious gifts bestowed upon our lives by keeping a small box of life's teachings tucked ever so neatly upon our shelves, never to be discarded and only to be re-opened to remind us of God's miracle: the ability to clean out our closets, be grateful for all our treasures, and begin again.

In writing this book, I have "poked fun" at many of the peaks and valleys of life. It has been both cathartic and fun for me. My intentions were never to slight any phase of life or anyone else's personal story. Over the course of my life, I have experienced many aspects of human emotion and profound personal growth. As I head into the three-quarters turn in the race of life, I have chosen to reflect upon the distance behind me with levity. I offer this book to all of you, my gal pals, served on a platter of humor and garnished with many chuckles.

It is my hope as you read this fictional quip about life's trials, tribulations, and adventures that you will all find some pieces, if not chunks, that are very familiar. We all go through "stuff" in our lives, mistakenly believing we are the only ones. Well, I am here to tell you that you are not alone. If we could take a peek into each other's closets at this very moment, we would see similar "Been There, Done That, Bought the T-Shirt" tees in various colors and sizes. Often times, many have been through so much worse.

If I accomplish anything great with this book, I hope it will be laughter. My sense of humor kept me going when I didn't think I could muster up the strength emotionally or physically to continue. The real intention of this book is to provide solace and encouragement to all of you, so that together we may continue the remainder of life's race with a smile on our faces, the wind at our backs, and "Pedaling as Fast as We Can."

Sandra Joan Mullen

You grow up on the day you have your first real laugh at yourself.

—Ethel Barrymore

NOTE: This is a work of fiction. Names, characters, places, and incidents either are the product of the author's imagination and/or are used fictitiously. Any resemblance to actual persons, living or dead, business establishments, events, or locales is entirely coincidental.

The Beginning

MY SCHOOL GIRL FANTASY: THE JETSONS

I am Jane Jetson. Like Jane Jetson, I am voluptuous. But unlike the popular Hanna-Barbera cartoon, I have a corporate agenda and the body of a runway model, outfitted in designer labels. It is seven ten a.m., and my five-foot, ten-inch slender yet athletically framed body is dressed to kill. I am wearing my favorite powder blue Chanel suit, Hermes silk scarf, and matching Etienne Aigner pumps, complemented by an exquisite Bric's of Italy leather attaché bag. As I run frantically out the twelve-foot etched glass double doors of my New York penthouse suite, I pause for a brief moment to kiss my George (Jetson), a Sean Connery look-alike, before taking the elevator to the rooftop to catch the monorail to work.

Halfway there, I suddenly realize that in my haste to get to my Wednesday morning board meeting, I have forgotten something. I immediately head back into the penthouse where Rosie, the live-in maid, is waiting with protein shake in hand and my two sharply uniformed and meticulously groomed children by her side. Yes, daughter Judy and my boy Elroy are patiently waiting for their mum's goodbye kisses. As I watch my children board their monorail to St. Uppercrust Prep School, I rush to catch mine.

As the new CEO of Jane's Sprockets, formerly Spacely's Sprokets, I am immediately greeted by all my adoring employees. I walk through the congestion of well-wishers and butt kissers to be greeted by my secretary Sven (got him from Kelly Boys). Did I fail to mention that he's gorgeous and has the most incredible hands? He was a masseur in his native country. His unbridled manual dexterity not only makes him one of the finest word processors alive but also endows him with the capability of making the most stressful workdays tolerable. Sven also makes a mean cappuccino. Oh, what a guy!

With Nespresso cappuccino in hand, I head up to my rooftop office. As the elevator doors open, I am reminded why I love this job. It's not just the six-figure income with its profit sharing bonuses, or the six-week vacation at the corporate villa in the south of France. The *piece de resistance* is my solid marble desk (imported from Italy) that faces a panoramic view of the New York City skyline. The mahogany walls of my office are adorned with Renaissance masterpieces and a plaque with the gold inlayed inscription *WWGD?* (What Would Gloria (Steinem) Do?). Oh, could I have envisioned anything better than this? Not in my most hallucinogenic schoolgirl fantasies.

I spend the bulk of my workday barraged with international business calls and warding off corporate takeovers. I even manage to sign a deal with the Chinese that will net my company one *bazillion* dollars in profit. All in one mover-and-shakers day's work.

As I head down the elevator to catch the monorail home, I check the time on my diamond pearl-faced Rolex watch. It is seven thirty. I am comforted by the thought that Rosie will have the children fed and bathed with homework done, ready to be tucked into bed when I arrive. It is Wednesday, which means rack of lamb, a bottle of vintage Sterling Merlot breathing, and George awaiting me with playful sex on his mind.

THE ABOVE HALLUCINOGENIC PROGRAMMING HAS JUST BEEN INTERRUPTED.

Chapter One

Flash Forward Twenty Years...

IN A NUTSHELL, REALITY SUCKS

I am lounging in REM sleep. Oh, what a wonderful dream! I am thirty-five years old, yet during this reincarnation, I have been blessed with the common sense and street smarts of someone who has lived a well-seasoned life of the good, bad, and ugly. Because this is my dream, I have bestowed upon myself the looks and body of a Victoria's Secret model, breasts and all.

Okay, by now, you have probably figured out that, unless I am in drag, I am not Clint Eastwood. I am a woman. But I am not just any woman. I am that lethal and much envied combination of beauty and brains. Oh, how I love this dream! Not only am I presented with this sleep-induced opportunity to rewind, but I am affording myself the tools to "catch eyes", kick ass and take names.

To my dismay, as I slip into my expensive, stylish, "ass kicking" shoes and leaf through the names in my "need to know" address book, I vaguely hear a disturbance echoing in my ears. This unwelcome noise becomes louder and louder with each passing second, making it increasingly difficult to concentrate on just how incredibly incredible I am. This is really starting to piss me off. This blaring noise is disturbing my blissful and somewhat (okay, probably totally) fantasizing slumber.

In an instant, much against my will, reality replaces REM. I am not Heidi Klum. I am the midlife, breast challenged, divorced mom of two. I am *Abagal Smart.* It is six a.m., and that horrible sound is my alarm clock awakening me to yet another forty-something–year-old day. Reality sucks!

I lethargically roll my athletically toned body (due to a masochistic five times a week work out regimen) over from my back to my side to begin the process of slowly, limb by limb, joint by joint, expelling myself from my warm womb (equipped with its own virtual reality). Oh, **footnote #1:** I changed my sleeping position from my right side to my back in an effort to camouflage the effects of gravity and birthing two children. My stomach may be somewhat wider, but the back position still affords that concave appeal. As I place my size eight feet on the floor, which have also become slightly wider due to the added weight of carrying these very healthy babies, I am extremely proud of the fact that not only can I see my feet, but, with acute detail, I can also see my well pedicured toes with their cleverly appointed toe rings and fluorescent fuchsia nail color. Ah, the miracle of science: Lasik surgery. Amazingly, this scientific wonder has transpired without the slightest squint of my deep blue eyes.

Aimlessly I walk into my bathroom, catching a glimpse of myself in the mirror. I pace back and forth, dizzily glancing at my maturing caricature, assembling my Spandex attire and Adidas sneakers for my morning run. Quite reflexively, my eyes flash to my bathroom counter laden with age defying or is that denying spackles, ointments, and creams.

Slowly, my brain's memory synapses begin to fire. Now I remember—yes, it's all coming back to me. I started subscribing or is it prescribing to these antidotes approximately eight years ago (precipitated by my fortieth birthday). I remember waking up one morning totally perplexed by the newfound creases in my forehead and between my brows. After a few months, I depressingly realized I hadn't just slept funny. Yes, it was just another one of those "Reality Sucks" moments.

As I begin to examine every detail of the face and the body of the woman who birthed two children, gave most of her adult life to one man, and recently endured a metamorphosis physically, mentally and emotionally I commence my self-analyzing routine. "Am I pleased with the woman who is looking back at me? Is this woman hugging (or more accurately white knuckling) the final bend of midlife successful? Unconsciously, my use of the term *successful* begs yet more questioning: "What characterizes "successful" and how do I measure up to this self-induced definition?" This early morning self-analyzation elicits flashbacks of the past forty-eight years. Could this be an after effect of the excessive consumption of those "organic" brownies in college? I just knew I shouldn't have gone back for seconds.

IT'S A WONDERFUL LIFE?

Chapter Two

SO MANY QUESTIONS, SO LITTLE TIME

I spend the remainder of my week wrestling with this fantasy vs. reality dichotomy, naively hoping this reflection might provide an accurate barometer of how well I am doing so far. It seems I now require a benchmark to ensure that what I seek for the balance of my life remains in check. Frustratingly, the early morning, bathroom mirror flashbacks have begun consuming my preciously rare quiet moments. With each flashback, I become increasingly cognizant of a harsh truth. What I have become and where I am today is a slightly (I am being selfishly kind) altered rendition of what I once envisioned. Not only has my school girl, Jane Jetson hallucination been thrown to the curb, but my recent Victoria's Secret REM sleep dream has proved to be nothing more than that. This reality plagues me with more self-questioning. "Who is this forty-something-year-old woman I sometimes grudgingly acknowledge as me, *Abagal Smart*? What has she accomplished with her life? What can she still hope to be when she finally grows up?"

With my work schedule, the demands of two teenage children, and this latest preoccupation with the meaning of life, the week, much like the last forty-eight years, flies by. It is now a chilly Friday evening, the kids are with their dad and I have the entire weekend to myself. I am curled up in my favorite overstuffed La-Z-Boy recliner, a bit misplaced in my beautifully appointed, classically traditional living room, with a glass of my favorite vintage Sterling Merlot (some fantasies remain intact) in hand. As the sun sets on yet another forty-something-year-old day, I gaze catatonically at the last burning embers of a once blazing fire in my massive river rock fireplace and question myself out loud (here I go again), "Where in the H-E-double toothpicks did the last forty-eight years go?"

At one time, it seemed the childhood and adolescence stage was endless. I spent that awkward and somewhat painful period of my life preoccupied with thoughts and fantasies of being older, more beautiful, smarter, finding the right guy (sometimes just any guy), and securing the "white picket fence" life. Then, as if flashed forward via warp speed, "beam me up Scotty," I was transported into midlife, a stage that offers two guarantees: wrinkles and hair dye. Okay, if I count that my breasts have begun gravitating toward my armpits, there are three. In what seems like one long winter's night, I have gone from pimples to wrinkles.

Is there no mercy? Actually, it's far worse! I have been hit by the "no mercy stick" twice. I am blessed with what our beauty experts (who are these damn people?) refer to as "combination skin." I have pimples *and* wrinkles! I am convinced that Mother Nature is a dominant shareholder in the corporations that manufacture both Clearasil and Alpha Hydroxy.

Now, more than ever, it does seem that the mature period of life overshadows youth. The omnipotence of youth is replaced by a philosophical preoccupation with the whos, whats, whens and wheres. Oh, what I wouldn't do for a mystical potion that would allow me to relive some earlier stage of my life, knowing what I know now! For me that magic age would be thirty-five years young.

As I meander through the midlife zone (some days, it seems like the twilight zone), reflection becomes a major aspect of my quiet moments. It's the moments of contemplation that lie somewhere between the end of the day and just before a sleep-induced coma. I recently rented an extremely profound movie entitled *Life as a House*. In this movie, the main character, portrayed by Kevin Kline, declares, "Hindsight is nothing more than foresight without a future." Wow! It is this woulda, coulda, shoulda mentality with its stinging precision that envelops this stage of life.

Footnote #2: I've also begun using this imaginary measuring stick. So, sticking (no pun intended) with a movie theme, I would have to say on one end of my life's measuring stick is *It's A Wonderful Life* and on the other end is *As Good As It Gets.*

With this analogy in place, I feel an overwhelming need to summon my favorite elephant flannel "jammies" and piggy slippers and slip underneath my comfy king-sized duvet. I mosey into the kitchen, grab my bowl of Orville Redenbacher popcorn, my stashed box of Snowcaps, and the bottle of Sterling and head upstairs to the warmth and solitude of my very own master (mistress?) suite. I am long overdue. It is time to settle down for a long winter's night of reflection.

Lying quietly, basking in the warmth and security that only very well-worn flannel (you know, the kind with the nubs) and junk food can conjure, I willingly let my mind wander and ponder, "Could God be a woman? Is she Gloria Steinem?"

Oh, sorry, wrong night. There goes that Prozac withdrawal thing again. **Footnote # 3:** I've voluntarily taken myself off Prozac. It left me wanting nothing. Yuk! Yuk! (A mature ha! ha!) I really need to speak to my herbal guy about this. Maybe I could wean ever so gradually with the aide of St. John's Wort. Okay, I am back on track. I am really pondering, "Where exactly am I on my imaginary continuum?" I quickly realize the answer to this much sought after midlife question is quite complex. No easy multiple-choice answer here. Regrettably, this answer will not come to me like a bolt of lightning just because my winter's night is just right. The true measure of where we are in life is found in where we've been. It is the journey. So, here I go! Gals, put on your favorite jammies, grab your junk food du jour and come along with me. I know the ride will be all too familiar. As my eye lids grow heavy and my mind begins to fade into slumber, I vaguely hear your echoes ringing in my ears: "Been There, Done That, Bought the T-Shirt."

A Long Winter Night's Dream

A FLASHBACK

Chapter Three
GROWING UP

I was raised in an average dysfunctional family. **Footnote #4:** I was truly disheartened by the realization we really didn't have the corner on this. I had always been led to believe we were anything but average.

My three brothers and I were Catholic hybrids. We were a genetic mutation, reproduced via a divorced Irish Catholic egg and a never-before-married English Protestant sperm. My mom carried the dominant gene, resulting in slightly watered down Catholic offspring. This by true definition is a "churchgoing Catholic" who believes the "host" is best complemented with a glass of fine red wine, preferably a cab or merlot.

My mother's parents were an integral part of our lives. Although my grandparents didn't reside with us, the umbilical cord stretched no more than one mile in all directions. We were much like military children in that we continually moved, transferred not by a Hummer but by my extended family's beckoning.

My grandmother was the matriarch. She ran her family business like an Irish mafia. She wanted the family in her apron pockets; if you didn't show for Sunday dinner, you were dead! It didn't take my brothers and me long to realize this family obligation was truly a blessing. My grandmother and aunt were wonderful cooks, and to our dismay, our mother had not inherited their culinary gene. **Footnote # 5:** I was a young adult before I knew the term "homemade" was not referring to the art of adding your own can of tuna to "Tuna Helper" or baking cookies with those perfect pumpkin appliqué centers. Truth be known, my mother's believed culinary skill had been stolen from Betty Crocker and that cute, giggly little doughboy.

All in all, we were the recipe for a fairly happy, loving, Cleaver-like family, mixed with a dash of the Sopranos, shaken, not stirred, and garnished with sprigs of the Addams Family. When served, this concoction delivered a walloping punch of family chemistry.

My fondest childhood memories center around our maroon, wood paneled station wagon and our cottage on Pre-Pubescent Lake. My adventures in the station wagon served me well in life's later conflicts and negotiations. My older brother and I would spend the majority of the family road trips fighting with each other and antagonizing our two younger brothers. I would then spend the rest of the ride defending myself and bartering with my father for a lesser punishment. My older brother, who was not as verbally eloquent, just got cracked.

Days at our lake cottage were equally educational. I learned to water-ski behind our family speedboat and received an honorary degree in mature male anatomy: I spent many a nine-year-old's morning inconspicuously peering through a small gap in the bedroom door at my handsome uncle's maleness as he dressed for breakfast. Since he was only related to me by marriage, it didn't seem quite as sacrilegious. I think it was this lack of bloodline that truly kept me from hell or at least from going blind.

At the ripe old age of twelve, I encountered the first of life's many letdowns. By virtue of my long, lanky, five-foot, ten-inch body frame, the center forward position on my middle school's basketball team and an athletic scholarship seemed inevitable. After one grueling week of conditioning and tryouts, I, Olive Oyl (as I was fondly referred to by both friends and family), earned the coveted position on the junior varsity team. However, after one lackluster season, it was blatantly apparent neither height nor a brawn boyfriend who had an insatiable appetite for spinach was enough. I came to terms with a depressing fact: I was scholastically adept and athletically inept. Brains, not a basketball, were my only hope of securing a college scholarship. As I slithered off the basketball court, my tail between my long, lanky, forever to be underutilized legs, and took one last glance at the scoreboard, I thought to myself, *You know, someone should enlighten these abundantly "testosteroned" female coaches. Olive Oyl or not, it's physically impossible to reach for a jump ball with one's cosmetic mirror and favorite ice pink lipstick in tow.* But now that I think about it, did those particular women ever apply lipstick? Hmm.

At about twelve and three-fourths, I discovered the second of life's injustices…the break up of my parents. Under my middle-income, Midwestern ranch roof, Love American Style had been canceled and replaced with Divorce Court and the anti-Cleavers. My once average dysfunctional family became a smidgen more dysfunctional.

Chapter Four

THE BIRDS, THE BEES, AND ALL THAT OTHER NONSENSE

ERA, burning bras, breaking glass ceilings, unified marches, Gloria Steinem… Oh, those were the days. I was just flirting with puberty when all these events transpired. With the breakup of my family, stand-ins were now playing the roles of Ward and June Cleaver. My new mother was a hybrid of Diane Keaton in *Looking for Mr. Goodbar* and Liz Taylor (needed to marry all the men she slept with), and my new father was a "Father Knows Best" with a corporate agenda. But because Dad had been exiled from the family camp due to infidelity (which at forty-eight, I am still trying to decipher), he was left, according to my Goodbar/Taylor mom and the chain of command (her family), with the inability to really know best.

As I ambled through puberty, my home life left me somewhat empty and without direction. My father moved into a makeshift apartment and my mother moved my three brothers and me to a modest house in a nice Italian Catholic neighborhood. Oh my! Nice *and* Italian Catholic? This was an oxymoron in this neighborhood! Not only had my mother been excommunicated from the church, but as soon as the wide-hipped, rosary-toting Italian wives got wind that a beautiful Irish divorcee with four fairly mischievous children had settled into the house on the corner of Spaghetti Avenue and Meatball Lane, she was excommunicated from the neighborhood as well. It was not pretty. If this had been Salem in the seventeenth century, we would have prayed for a shortage of stakes and matches!

I soon realized I needed a cause, something to preoccupy my consuming paranoia of being burnt at the stake. Ever so productively, I set my sights on the "women's movement." I was ready for the battle of the sexes! I was willing and somewhat able to burn my very own bra! With heavy heart, much consideration and trepidation, I decided that a 32AAAA trainer bra would just not suffice for a cause as serious as this. I presumed the lack of volume alone would earn me, at most, one-half a women's lib credit, which I was sure, would forbid me access to the secret handshake and keep me from being taken seriously by the rest of the gals.

Yet, I was determined. It would take a lot more than size inadequacy to discourage me. Gloria Steinem remained my heroine. I felt like Dorothy in *The Wizard of Oz*, and Gloria was my Glenda, the Good Witch of the North. I just knew, with Gloria at my side, those ruby slippers were within my grasp and there would be no place like…the top.

I set a strict course for the rest of my primary and secondary education, knowing full well a whole new world was out there, just waiting for *moi*. "Look up in the sky, it's a bird, it's a plane, it's…Super Corporate Woman." Primary education courses such as typing, shorthand, dictation, home-ec, and other such fossilized skills were cast aside and replaced with advanced math, science, and various business courses. My previous basketball career (ha ha) had taught me a valuable lesson: reach high, never let them see you sweat, and at all costs never mess up your "do."

Okay, before you hate me for my determination and focus, pull in those talons. Like all fairy tales, there were a few forks—or is that dorks—in the road. At this point in my life, my estrogen engorged glands took over and common sense began running a good five laps behind my sexual preoccupation. I had become an "I'm too sexy for my own good" girl; and a "bad boy," a Volkswagen, and a legal drinking age of eighteen momentarily derailed my best made plans.

I can vividly remember my most poignant initiation into the adult world; learning about the act of *sexual intercourse*. I was in Mrs. Doright's sixth grade sexual education class. For me, this experience was as traumatic as finding out there really wasn't a Santa Claus, Easter Bunny, or Tooth Fairy. My childhood innocence comprised of a stork, a bundle of joy, and a basket delivered to the front doorstep had been replaced by this repugnant vision of "copulation." **Footnote #6:** My cherished childhood memories of a Santa Claus, an Easter Bunny, and the Tooth Fairy would later be exchanged for brandied eggnog, faux rabbit fur coats, and crowned teeth. The loss of one's virginity is expected, but the loss of one's idealism is quite another matter. It really is for the birds, so to speak!

As I sat at my desk at Immaculate Conception Elementary School staring at still slides of the male and female anatomy and the "up too close and way too personal" union of the two, I can remember thinking, *This seems like a very high price to pay to carry on the family tree. What in the name of...would have possessed my parents to do this nasty deed four times?* I found the whole procreation thing revolting, not to mention extremely messy. Swapping spit was one thing, but other bodily fluids? Yuk! Shouldn't there at least be a bowl of hot water, lemons, and a twelve-hundred-thread count washcloth on the nightstand?

Fortunately, or unfortunately, my take on this subject did not last. At eighteen years old, I became hormonally abundant and fell madly in love with an older man; a sparsely bearded guy two years my senior whose last name sounded like something you planted in a vegetable garden. After a fine (1975 high school vintage) bottle of Boone's Farm Strawberry Hill wine, I lost my virginity watching *The Exorcist* (apropos) at the drive-in movie show in the back seat of his 1968 Volkswagen. Even more atrocious, imagine the picture of a five-foot, ten-inch, all legs girl (or as my grandfather lovingly put it, I had legs up to my ass) with a six-foot, four-inch, equally long-legged guy "doing it" in the back seat. We depicted the mating dance of two daddy long-legs spiders. At one point in this clumsy union, I believe I saw my orange neon painted toes in the back seat of the Chevy Malibu parked in front of us. Who said lovemaking was romantic? I lathered Ben Gay on my muscles and joints for a week following this fiasco.

I spent the next several years begging the question "Is this all there is?" It took many more years of experience and mature love to successfully provide the answer.

Chapter Five

BACK ON TRACK

After graduating from high school with highest honors and my inevitable breakup with Mr. "Something You Planted in the Vegetable Garden," I decided it was time to gain my independence. I cut the umbilical cord and moved out. At nineteen, I left my Goodbar/Taylor mom, the rest of my anti-Cleaver family, and the wide-hipped, rosary toting neighborhood to take up digs with an estranged—or was that strange—aunt (my mother's old maid, "still virginal" sister) who called Sticksville and a white clapboard house with a front porch and a swing *home*.

I boarded a jet plane with my childhood doll, Sweetie Baby, and a three-month supply of birth control pills and headed for the hills, so to speak. I was departing my birthplace, a suburb of a city that had produced such soul legends as Aretha Franklin, Smokey Robinson, and Diana

Ross, bound for this rural Southern town where nothing—not an armadillo, not watching Vanna White turn letters seven nights a week with my eccentric aunt, and not even the occasional overindulgence in mint juleps—would distract me from my educational goals.

I was once again possessed with success and myopically focused on my higher education. My secondary education at the renowned University of Sticksville was composed of accounting, finance, marketing, and computer courses, all paving the way for one dynamo corporate woman, hell bent on CEOdom.

I spent most of my lucid hours taking eighteen credit hours of college courses working for straight A's, and the majority of my nights waiting tables at the local restaurant/bar. I quickly realized that what I hadn't learned about life on the high school basketball court I was now obtaining in an establishment that served mass quantities of alcohol to monster truck driving, tobacco chewing, gun- and-dog-toting specimens of men. At times, I debated whether my brief basketball career or this experience better equipped me for the real world. I was amazed at what I was willing to subject myself to for mediocre tips and a fair to middling—or was that swampland—education. By the time I crawled into bed at night, usually about three a.m., I would spend the remaining minutes of my day, just before falling into a sleep induced coma, fantasizing (probably from sleep deprived delirium) about my future (my Jane Jetson schoolgirl fantasy).

Okay, girls, let's face it. We were doomed from the minute Mom took us to see *Cinderella*. From that moment on, our heads were polluted with the warped melody of "Someday My Prince Will Come," forcing us to live out the fairy tale or at least fantasize trying. I've heard there are phenomenal drugs available for women who are not innately equipped with these skills. In hindsight, I should have succumbed to such antidotes. I would have made a perfect Stepford wife. Okay, okay…after breast augmentation, some cooking lessons, and a series of collagen treatments.

After witnessing my slightly altered Cleaver family transform into *Meet the Fockers*, I really was somewhat shell shocked about the whole finding Prince Charming, falling in love, and that happily ever after thing. Could I find the white picket fence life I had always fantasized about? Where did I begin and how? The fact that I now resided in a county whose eligible bachelors' first names were all a Bubba or Bo derivative, and whose idea of a white horse was the latest series John Deere tractor, threw a huge monkey wrench into my fairy tale. To complicate matters, my ball gown was at the cleaners and I still couldn't find one of my glass slippers. I was doomed!

Even so, I was a twenty year old mover and shaker in the collegiate world. I was driven to make my mark as a very successful businesswoman. Quite unlike my mother, I could aptly take care of myself without a man. The only man I deemed worthy of my attention would drive a convertible foreign sports car (my twentieth-century version of a white horse), live in a large beautifully appointed home (my castle), and be extremely successful in his own right (heir to the throne). This was my definition of Prince Charming, and nothing less would veer me off course.

Chapter Six

LIVING OUT THE FAIRY TALE: ENTER THE FRANK LLOYD WRIGHT OF PICKET FENCES

Life is truer than fiction. I managed to find Bobby…my very own "Bobby Ewing." He drove a Japanese sports car and lived on Sticksville's version of South Fork. My "Dallas" Prince Charming was president and co-owner of a fence company. His specialty was designing white picket fences. This man, a few years my senior, appeared to have all the right stuff, and to my grandmother's delight was Irish Catholic to boot.

After eleven months of frenzied courtship including two county fairs, three rodeos, going "mudding," and a trip to Disney World, Bobby and I were married.

As the first wedding in our brand new Catholic Church, our marriage was blessed by a priest and a precarious mixture of Union and Confederate family and friends. It was a typical steamy, sticky, Southern summer day. Ninety-eight degrees, one hundred percent humidity, malfunctioning air conditioning, a close call with the symbolic union of three lighted candles and a designer wedding dress, and a passed out groom gave a new twist to the seventh sacrament! Looking back, I should have realized this was a sign, or more aptly a brazen omen.

At twenty-one, what do you really know about marriage, maintaining the fairy tale, or for that matter just keeping up the castle? Other than *All My Children*, Harlequin Romance novels, and Dow's "scrubbing bubbles," I was clueless. How much could a husband expect from a new wife who had only recently realized you were supposed to remove the concealed bags of "stuff" from the Thanksgiving turkey (don't forget the neck cavity, too) before you cooked it? I quickly learned an invaluable lesson: over promise and under deliver. I think I had it backwards. I am a tad dyslexic. I am sure this confusion or condition was a contributing factor to my inevitable marital demise.

The first several years of our union were occupied by the completion of my college education (bachelor's and master's degrees) and ironing out minor details such as which way the toilet paper roll should go (anyone knows it's flipped over the top), whether the toothpaste should be squeezed from the end or the center (anyone knows it's the center because you get to the bottom in the end), and whose family was weirdest (hands down, it was his). I had come to terms with my role as Eva Gabor in *Green Acres*. I learned to accept my place in Sticksville, but "darling, I longed for Park Avenue!"

Amazingly eight years transpired. For someone with poor standards of what a good marriage should be and who despairingly utilized the self-help book with the large print entitled, "Keeping Your Prince Charming for Dummies," I was doing pretty damn well.

However, I began to recognize that my corporate aspirations were being quickly checked at the front door—or was that the white picket fence gate? This rural Southern area, which produced such success for my husband, left me with two career choices: an extremely overqualified okra picker or joining the family fence business. With my fair Irish skin, my phobic fear of hard manual labor, and the possibility of breaking an acrylic nail, I chose the latter.

All was seemingly well with my career choice. Other than the fact that I detested the co-owner, my father-in-law, my corporate agenda was being minimally met. I knew that given enough time, like any family run business, my day would come with the retirement or death of the V.P. Didn't the Southern states produce Oleander to expedite such occasions?

Waiting for "Psycho Daddy" to step down from his throne left me extremely disillusioned, depressed, and unfulfilled, however. I was a frustrated CEO wannabe. As an escape, I began concentrating on building a new house with a one-of-a-kind, designer picket fence and the possibility of extending our family tree. It was mutually (from my point of view) decided that our D.I.N.K (double income, no kids), selfish lifestyle needed to be replaced with Yuppiedom, green wood paneled minivan and all.

Chapter Seven

THE HARD BOILED EGG

With the career thing looking fairly bleak, I decided to spend my time and energy adding to the royal lineage. Besides, we would eventually need fresh blood to run the fence business or plow the back "forty." After eight years, it was time to get us pregnant! I was ready to turn in my barely used Bric's of Italy attaché for a state of the art Land's End diaper bag.

After what seemed like a gazillion years, I quit taking my birth control pills and began having sex on a regular basis, like Bobby and I used to do before life interrupted the lustful, sex-crazed part of the relationship. I set our sights and lovemaking calendar on *ovulation!*

It didn't take but three ovulation cycles for me to come to a reality check. This baby-making thing was a whole lot of work. Who were these women who got pregnant on their wedding nights? Were they freaks of nature or those wide-hipped, Catholic Italian women from my childhood neighborhood? Were some women born to birth and others born to try?

After one year of assuming every possible position, including standing on my head in the corner of the bedroom (all I got was a headache and that seemed to defeat the purpose) and witnessing three doves break their little necks flying into my bedroom window (a Catholic mother wannabe's worst nightmare), I thought it might be time to seek out some divine intervention. I called my gynecologist and asked her to recommend a local fertility god or, more commonly known in the hardboiled egg circles, an infertility specialist.

After one consultation, Bobby and I realized there was much more to this than birds and bees. This trying to make a baby thing was much more complex and grueling than my first experience in the back of the Volkswagen, which now seemed like a lifetime and many different shades of fluorescent toenail polish ago. Was this my penance for making my career a priority and wasting all that money trying not to get pregnant?

Bobby and I also quickly understood just how naïve I was concerning the male sexual anatomy. Evidently, I hadn't been paying as much attention as I'd thought I was in Mrs. Doright's sixth grade sex education class. Maybe it was a day I was preoccupied with what was on the hot lunch menu in the cafeteria. I knew my obsession with food would get me in trouble one day. I didn't get fat, but I sure was sexually retarded.

If someone wrote a medical order for a sperm test, wouldn't you envision a sterile lab and some form of extraction device? Never in my most horrific nightmares did I envision a plastic specimen cup and a public restroom. If I had contemplated this reality, I would have stopped at the local drug store and picked up a *Penthouse* magazine for my husband and a Valium prescription (the eighties Prozac) for me. As I watched a pale, humiliated Bobby cross the crowded waiting room with his sterile vial in tow, I quickly turned up the volume on the waiting room television to drown out any possibility of noise that might erupt from the very conspicuous bathroom.

After a month of lengthy tests, we came to the conclusion that most of the pregnancy dysfunction was due to me. I had severe endometriosis and low levels of progesterone. However, just to be sure we were covering all our bases, I went out and bought my husband a wide variety of boxer shorts in various colors and patterns, pitching his briefs for the benefit of stronger swimmers (sperm). Unsubstantiated scientific theory stated that boxers allowed the family jewels to hang free and cool, allowing greater potential of producing Olympic hopefuls. The vision of these little guys in their Speedos competing for the prize warmed my little eggs' hearts.

So, hand in hand, Bobby and I began our journey down Infertility Lane. After several complicated surgeries, various tried and true fertility drugs, and a high-tech ovulation predictor kit, I became intimate friends with a big blue dot, sterile vials for sperm transportation, stirrups, and a butterfly appliqué on my doctor's procedure room ceiling. An experience that once invoked considerable pleasure now became my new and very demanding career. Bobby never knew whom he was having sex with due to the Cybil-like personality produced by the infertility drugs. If I had worn different colored wigs and spoken in tongues, maybe he would have been more tolerant.

All our hard work paid off. By the time I was thirty-six years old, we had two lovely children. One side effect of our infertility saga was the Pavlov's dog reaction Bobby experienced every time he got a phone call in the middle of the day. This so-called erectile "function" dissipated as soon as he heard the screaming children in the background. We soon were back in step with the sexual normalcy of new parents: once every month on Sunday, very quietly, during the children's naps with the baby monitor on the nightstand.

Another side effect was my newfound skin. The first time I bent over to pick up the toilet paper I'd dropped while sitting on the commode, I was met with layers of freshly rolled flesh. I lost the added baby weight and my skin lost its elastic memory. What had happened to Olive Oyl? Between two babies, my size six body had adequately stretched to accommodate a weight gain of approximately one hundred pounds. Okay, my babies only weighed 6.6 lbs. and 8.8 lbs. respectively. Much to my embarrassment, the rest was the residual of Nestle Toll House cookies, Subway's loaded tuna subs, and party sized bags of Lay's potato chips.

The most negative side effect of childbearing was losing bladder control. Just uttering the words *toilet paper* and *commode* in the same sentence elicits my own Pavlov's dog response: a warm tingly feeling down there and the uncontrollable need to take a potty break. It isn't fair! I was a good pregnant patient. I practiced my Kegels. I would spend twenty minutes on the toilet daily, tightening, releasing, tightening, releasing. During one of my Kegel marathons, in the last trimester of my pregnancy, when my size alone left me completely out of breath, Bobby, hearing me breathing loudly and heavily, yelled from the bedroom, "Honey, come back to bed. I can do that for you and I promise it will be a whole lot more fun."

Men are so insensitive. Didn't Mr. Smartass realize it was this attitude that had put me on the toilet doing these humiliating exercises to begin with? When all was said and done, I admit I did benefit slightly from all my Kegel efforts. **Footnote #7:** I don't pee my pants at the drop of a jumping jack but I can set my watch by my potty break intervals.

Chapter Eight

THE UNRAVELING OF THE AMERICAN DREAM

By the time the new millennium rolled around, most people were obsessed with thoughts and fears of technological meltdowns of cosmic proportion. I, on the other hand, was consumed with my failing marriage and the shocking realization that my dreams of yesteryear had become today's nightmare.

My schoolgirl, Jane Jetson fantasy of monorails, Rosie, corporate takeovers, finely appointed children, and Sean Connery were being replaced by earth shattering, mind-altering reality. As I rolled over in bed one morning to turn off the alarm, instead of finding a ravaged naked body, leftover from the previous night's sexual escapade, I was horrified to discover my body completely clothed in a Christmas Holly flannel nightgown and granny panties. You know the ones. You can pull them up high enough to meet the undersides of your newly gravity challenged breasts. At that moment, I was a Victoria's Secret dropout. My own reality was shocking enough, but the nightmare continued when I glanced across the bed and was met by what looked like a stubbly Alfred E. Newman. Not finding Sean was one thing, but where had my Bobby Ewing gone? This stranger yelled out a few profane words and began scratching himself in that conspicuous area all men like to scratch first thing in the morning. Yes, my husband of twenty-one years had somehow become Alfred E. Newman with an attitude and what appeared to be a good case of the crabs.

I ran around the house confused and totally dismayed. What had happened to my life? Yes, my South Fork ranch was still large and beautifully appointed…okay, this was a good sign. What about my perfect children? I entered my son's room and found him peacefully sleeping. I sat down on the edge of his bed and began affectionately running my hand through the back of his hair. With each loving stroke, I began to catch my breath. As I lowered my head to give him a subtle kiss on the back of his neck, I realized his cute freckled birthmarks were beginning to look more like three conspicuously placed sixes. Immediately, I was brought to my knees. Residuals of lethargically practiced Catholicism kicked in and I began a rambling rendition of the Act of Contrition. Where was my rosary? It was packed away in the attic along with my first trainer bra, my "Your First Menstruation" kit and my First Holy Communion prayer book in a box labeled "Firsts". Right before my eyes, my son was transforming into the Anti-Christ. In utter panic, I ran to my daughter's room. Oh no! Instead of finding my precious thirteen year old daughter, I found this woman wannabe sitting straight up in bed with eyes rolled back into her head. Her head began spinning in a full 360 and she began chanting, "I hate my life, my hair looks like crap, and I have absolutely nothing to wear!" My fantasy Jetson children, daughter Judy and my boy Elroy, had become Wednesday and Pugsley of the Addams Family.

Realizing I was living a nightmare, I ran to my attaché case to get my Prozac (only recently invented). Oh no, could it be? My fine leather Bric's of Italy was a nine-year-old, extremely well-worn, once state of the art, Land's End diaper bag, monogrammed with the fading, barely legible initials M.O.M.

As I headed to the kitchen to find something to chase down the Prozac, like a dirty martini (with olives, shaken, not stirred), I was met by a Thelma Ritter look-alike with instant coffee and a chocolate Pop Tart, not my fantasy robot maid Rosie with a protein shake. In what seemed like one long night's dream, my corporate equation to Dorothy and the ruby slippers, Gloria Steinem, and Glenda the Good Witch of the North had become a Wicked Witch of the West, bucket of water, total Oscar-worthy meltdown.

FOR SALE

Chapter Nine

WHAT WAS I THINKING?

Where was Gloria Steinem? Was she not partially responsible for this travesty? Where was my bra? Maybe it wasn't too late to retrieve it from the incinerator. I'd never taken advantage of breast augmentation, so I was sure it still fit. I had been duped. There had to be an attorney who would represent me in a class action suit for "wrongful life" or better yet "wrongful wife"! I screamed hysterically, irrationally hoping my ERA gal pals would hear me. "Take back your decoder rings, your women's lib credits, and I promise never to divulge the secret handshake! I've changed my mind. I don't want to be Ms. "Mover and Shaker. I want to be Mrs. June Cleaver after all!"

After twenty-one years of keeping up this charade, I was exhausted! What had happened to evolution? According to that theory, weren't all species supposed to adapt to changes in their environment over time? It had been over thirty years since the ERA movement and that totally ridiculous commercial about bringing home the bacon and frying it up in the pan. Let's face it: male homo sapiens were just not living up to their adaptation function. Had I reinforced Bobby's belief that it was humanly (womanly) possible to wear all these hats and still have time to "never let him forget he's a man?" Forget petitioning Congress for year round Daylight Savings Time, I needed a twenty-eight hour day. I just knew I would learn to regret not succumbing to the Stepford wife thing. I'd learned the fence business; couldn't he learn to vacuum? I had fairly astute math skills, but even utilizing the new math, this was definitely not a fifty-fifty partnership. Actually, it could have been more accurately labeled indentured servitude.

In the years prior to our children, Bobby and I spent our evenings having fabulous dinners (which we both took turns preparing), drinking a wonderful bottle of wine and sharing intimate conversations about our future. Now we sat across the dinner table from each other with two additional guests, a Dominos pizza and a gallon jug of "on sale" Burgundy and debated who was more exhausted. Honestly, it was me!

Why couldn't my husband, whom I had been married to longer than most criminals get for murder, get the fact that I had turned into a "huswife;" this melding of a husband and wife. I had become June Cleaver juggling all the balls—or was that *with* "balls"? He had just stayed plain ole Ward. I was the Worker Bee with the continued expectation of my Queen Bee role of maintaining the hive. I needed a wife of my very own, before I came to the revelation that I could do this less grudgingly on my own. At least if I went solo, I could find more productive ways to spend the last fifteen minutes of my day than coming up with fresh creative excuses for being too tired for sex.

Speaking of sex, more so romance, I couldn't remember the last time Bobby had said I was beautiful, sexy, or even that he adored me and couldn't live without me. When was the last time he casually walked by me and patted me lovingly on the butt or affectionately kissed the back of my neck? Okay, in all fairness, maybe that isn't the first thing that comes to a man's mind when he is met by a woman in elephant flannel "jammies" and piggy slippers.

I had to acknowledge my part in this meltdown and bear some of the blame. When was the last time I told Bobby he was handsome, my Bobby Ewing, or that he was everything to me? Just because he had a paunch, a receding hairline, and after twenty-one years had exceeded his inalienable male right to scratch his "jewels" first thing in the morning, was I justified in my desire for a trade-in?

My "once upon a time" Prince Charming had become equally disillusioned. He had lost all interest in his kingdom (South Fork), castle (the ranch), and obtaining the throne (taking over the fence business). In all my preoccupation with my own woulda, coulda, shouldas, I failed to realize that my prince had actually abdicated many years before. His father, the king, with all his unrealistic expectations had finally worn him down.

Our marriage needed intervention of a very desperate kind. Since neither one of our dysfunctional families offered much in the "how to save a failing marriage" column, I took charge as I always did and began a search for Sticksville's closest version of Dr. Phil.

The first $125 per hour session was allotted to hear Bobby's side of the story. However, quite selfishly, he never came back again to hear mine. I spent the next year trying to save our drowning marriage alone and coming to terms with never getting my turn.

Chapter Ten

BREAKING UP IS SO VERY HARD TO DO

As I headed into a brand new century, life, like my pubescent daughter, spun out of control. Unlike my daughter, however, my crisis had nothing to do with a bad hair day or the lack of cool clothes.

Bobby had walked out on me due to an email affair I was having with a Sean Connery impersonator. Just like my father many years previous, I too was exiled from the family camp due to imagined infidelity. Today, there would be considerable debate concerning the true definition of infidelity. The new millennium has produced numerous technological advances, altering the complexion of unfaithfulness. I never "bought the T-shirt" so to speak but nonetheless, I was guilty of adultery of the cyber space kind.

I was immediately terminated from my newly obtained V.P. position in the family fence business (yes, the nasty geezer finally stepped down). My ousting might have had something to do with the fact that Bobby was president. This was a fine example of "conflict of interest." I lost my Neimen Marcus, Saks, and Lord and Taylor credit cards, and my name was removed from all joint bank accounts and the white picket fence corporate marquee. I was reduced to groveling and begging for an allowance, which I earned by cooking dinner and sitting across the table from Bobby every night until the divorce was final. My spinster aunt had suggested a wonderful recipe for Oleander casserole. But, terminating my children's daddy did not seem in their psychological best interest. Besides that, the thought of wearing an orange jumpsuit (definitely not my color) embroidered with a black "Women's Correctional Facility" insignia was not in mine either. I opted for a little humble pie. After all, wasn't this my penance for being given the Internet version of the scarlet letter? They were now called cyber letters and could be purchased in different sizes and colors at a volume discount from eBay. If I had known it was going to turn out like this, I may have "bought the T-Shirt". At least my punishment would fit the crime. Was I really an Internet adulteress or just a pathetically lonely woman suffering from attention deficit (of the husband kind)?

By the summer of 2002, I had become a forty-four year old single woman who had been left with fifty percent of the responsibility of raising the children and somewhat less than that percentage of the marital assets. Quite unfairly, I didn't get my half of the vintage collection of John Deere tractors, the stock in the fence business, or the twelve place settings of fine china inlayed with eighteen carat gold deer figures, which we received as wedding gifts through Cabela's hunting catalog. My Christmas gifts of jewelry, furs, designer clothes, and perfume were totally out of the picture now. Instead my brand new ex-husband spent his time and money creating a very large wood-carved lawn figure and placed it in my "used to be" front yard for all to see. The cartoon-like figure held a neon sign which proclaimed, "The Grinch is Gone!!" And according to the local gossip was last seen in the projects or just off "skid row". I presumed this was located somewhere on the western side of Sticksville. As much as I tried to delude myself, I don't think Bobby or the town folk's fabricated (or was that wishful thinking) tale of "last seen locale" was referring to the green, fuzzy Dr. Seuss character. I just couldn't fathom that the father of my children and the "once upon a time" prince I loved was capable of this deed. My attorney, Sticksville's infamous F. Lee Clampett, predicted this immature "zinging." He explained that legal disputes bring out the best in the worst people (criminals) and the worst in the best people (divorcing couples). Yet, to my elation, this cute little decoration mysteriously disappeared "once upon a midnight dreary" and was never seen or heard from again. Hmm, I wonder who did that?

Chapter Eleven

REINVENTING THE MILLENNIUM GIRL

To even begin to fully understand the transformation that took place, you need to have an accurate picture of this newly divorced, extremely idealistic woman who was clueless about a world without a husband. For the past twenty-three years, I only knew the "white picket fence" life. I couldn't imagine what on earth I could do for a career in the seemingly godforsaken place where I lived that would enable even a modicum of similarity to my previous existence. Neither a Piggly Wiggly cashier nor okra picker commanded a six-figure income.

I envisioned myself searching the beauty supply aisle of Sticksville's Piggly Wiggly for L'Oreal auburn hair color, which hopefully matched Enrique's Posh Salon's no longer affordable, $180 shade. I was consumed with thoughts of enrolling myself in an acrylic, French manicure nail course and purchasing my "come f_ _ k me" pumps at Payless. As I contemplated such atrocities, my heart began to race, my breathing accelerated and I began to sweat profusely. Even though my sex life was going through a bit of a dry spell, I was quite sure, if my memory served me well, that what I was experiencing was not an orgasm. Damn! I calmed my anxiety attack by slowly breathing in and out of the last remaining Prada shoe bag hidden in the recesses of my newly rented condo closet. I briefly entertained the thought of becoming a high-class hooker, but I wasn't sure which corner of the street was labeled "geriatric" or what lewd and lascivious acts would be required to lure aging, potbellied, tobacco chewing Bo's and Bubba's away from their prized John Deere tractors. I quickly put that idea to rest.

Okay, girls: put away your rosaries and your boxes of tissues, this horror of horrors never transpired. I was saved by none other than "it's a bird, it's a plane, no it's Super Corporate Woman": tights, cape, big red letter "S" (no longer the scarlet one) and all. I may have "been there, done that" but I was Abagal Smart!

As I debated my obvious, or up to now, fairly well hidden talents, I found my career path: sales and marketing. I was a people person and over the years had managed to perfect the negotiation skills I had learned so well as a girl in the back of my dad's station wagon. I applied for a job at the local paper, *The Mullet Wrapper*. They offered me the position of classified sales manager which I gleefully accepted, knowing this would be right up my alley.

My midlife crisis had also changed the look of my post-childbearing body. The stress and depression that had accompanied this life-changing event brought me back to my teenage Olive Oyl shape. At forty-four years old, this skinny, somewhat athletically toned "size six" did not entirely complement my five-foot, ten-inch body. My face remained eye-catching but my body looked like a UNICEF commercial for world hunger. The breasts were now an even bigger problem. Actually, I don't think I would have considered them breasts anymore, just oversized areolas. Thank God for the Victoria's Secret's *Miracle*® bra. It afforded me the best of breasts devoid of a scalpel and anesthesia. I prayed for the prompt release of the next generation; Miracles of Miracles before the existing generation lost its support (literally). Victoria needed to quickly step up to the plate, or inevitably I would be forced to place my much-needed volume in Dr. Augmentation's hands.

Something I also hadn't counted on with my recent singleness was being ousted from the local "Society of Married Couples." Bobby managed to maintain his long standing membership, invitations to the annual Okra Harvest Festival, tractor pull tournaments, backyard BBQs, and all.

But this clannish group wanted nothing to do with me. As soon as the Fraternal Order of the Wives' Club, a sub-group of the Society, extracted the whole ugly and sordid divorce story from me, giving them enough material to keep them gossiping for at least the next thirty days, my membership was instantly revoked.

This was so déjà vu. Not much had changed with married women and their lack of acceptance of their newly divorced friends since my mother's experience more than thirty years ago. However, there were two facts these women failed to realize. I was both independent and intelligent and I definitely did not want any of their husbands! Yet, I could appreciate their concern. **Footnote # 8:** Given a *healthy* diet of Big Macs, French fries, strawberry shakes, and the latest generation of *Miracle*® bras, the entire "package" (face and body) could be quite attractive.

I had no idea what life was like on the outside in newly divorced, midlife dating world. I'd had, counting my best friend's brother, whom I felt sorry for because he was so shy, only three real boyfriends before my "Bobby Ewing." My sexual experiences were equally limited. It took me the better part of my early marriage to get over the compulsivity of the whole hot water, lemons, and the twelve-hundred-thread count washcloth on my nightstand after sex thing.

Yet, after months of being consumed with my new career, I began this preoccupation with the opposite sex. It was like high school. There were so many available men of all ages, sizes, colors, and personalities. I felt like I had been given the opportunity to be locked in a mall overnight and allowed to keep anything I could possibly grab before daylight. Even more miraculous, as I slowly adjusted to my new life and began adding much needed poundage; men began jumping into my shopping cart eagerly awaiting the checkout line. With the assistance of highly caloric protein shakes, I was regaining my fairly voluptuous (great butt and sultry legs) body. I felt like the forty-four year old Victoria Secret's model of Sticksville. Okay, I was still breast challenged, but I had a full set of teeth (with some prosthetic assistance) and I continued to look pretty damn good fully clothed. I had become so secure with my current standing that on any given night you could find me skipping out of Piggly Wiggly after seven p.m. happily humming the tune "I Feel Pretty." It was just what the doctor ordered. For the first time in a very long time, or maybe in my life, I felt like a real woman. I felt, yes, the infamous four letter word: **sexy**.

I am embarrassed to admit—no, that's a lie, I am actually thrilled to brag about my brief interlude with a man (okay, a boy) almost half my age. His name was Beauford. And yes, oh yes, much to my chagrin, they called him Bo for short. After three months of hot, steamy, unbridled (yes, there really was a barn and hay involved…you get the picture: lust), I terminated this torrid affair. He was brokenhearted. In my defense, my reasons were quite justifiable. I really do love Cream (the Eric Clapton band of the sixties) but not in my coffee, and I was growing weary of pretending my name really was Mrs. Robinson (*The Graduate*).

Shortly after my roll in the hay (pun totally intended) with Bo boy, I had a brief encounter with my Fertility God, Dr. Petri Dish. Let's face it, one of the most difficult aspects of getting back into the dating world (the saddle) again, other than what to wear on the first date, is having someone, other than the man you were married to for an eternity, see you naked. Well, who could be a better candidate than a man who not only had seen me naked but had examined, literally, every nook and cranny of my body inside and out and under the worst possible lighting; fluorescent? At this early stage of my singlehood, Dr. Petri Dish made a perfect guinea pig.

So, one gorgeous, warm, late summer, "not on call" day, a tennis attired Dr. Petri Dish showed up to my newly rented condo with flowers, a nice bottle of Chardonnay (I prefer a Merlot or a Cabernet) and swimming trunks for a quick game of tennis and a swim in the pool. Initially, I felt nervous and uncomfortable. I had never spoken to this man with my clothes on or without my feet in stirrups. Actually, I had not even conversed with him standing up.

However, with the progression of our day, I became more at ease with my Fertility God. He was actually very conversational, successfully managing to steer clear of my gynecological history and all work-related topics. As we lounged by the pool and finished off the bottle of Chardonnay, Dr. Petri Dish and I decided to cool down from our tennis match and the heat of the day with a dip in the pool.

As he emerged from the poolside bathroom in his swimming trunks, I was met by Chewbacca of Star Wars. Other than pictures of a Neanderthal man in my National Geographic's, I had never seen this much hair on any man. As he slowly lowered himself into the pool, I shockingly realized that not only could my Fertility God walk on water but the massive amounts of hair all over his body could as well.

I never had another date with Dr. Petri Dish. After what I had witnessed, I knew there was no future for us. I couldn't remotely entertain the prospect of having sex with him. I would exhaust Sticksville's supply of lint brushes in an effort to remove his hair from my silk sheets. I guess the old wives' tale is true. Men with meager amounts of hair on their heads more than make up for it with the hair on the remainder of their body.

After approximately six months of "trying on" a diverse assortment of men, I realized that, like a great outfit, I really wanted one that fit just right and complemented my style. Besides that, I could not physically or mentally continue. I was beginning to feel like that smiley yellow ball character at the local discount store, bouncing from one daily special to another. This recent obsession with men also began to interfere with my Saturday confessions at St. Celibacy Catholic Church. I was continually going over the allotted confession time limit. I ended up making a deal with Father No Carnal Knowledge that I would bring in dinner and a nice bottle of Merlot if he would supply the kneepads for my lengthy penances. This was a win/win for him. He got a delicious meal, a great bottle of wine, and an X-rated story without making dinner reservations or renting the movie.

Over the next two years, I slowed down this revolving door of men and began making major strides with the newspaper. I was responsible for increasing the advertising sales of my territory over twenty-five percent in the first year. By the second year, I was well on my way to being a classified super star!

Midway into my second year with the newspaper, however, I realized that I did not like working *for* someone. I had always worked for myself, so to speak. Even though it was alongside the Irish Godfather, sleeping with the President every night afforded incredible perks and an extremely flexible schedule. Now that I had shared custody of my two children, a nine-to-five job didn't allow time off if they were sick or to see my son play the part of Frosty the Snowman in the Christmas school play.

Shortly after returning from a wonderful Mediterranean cruise with my children, I decided it was time to become the mover and shaker I had always fantasized about. I became the first woman in the tri-county area or maybe in the entire state to become owner of a John Deere tractor franchise. Not too bad for an acrylic-nailed, Prada-shoed, Enrique-coiffed, Park Avenue "Eva Gabor."

The Bo's and Bubba's came from miles to see my inventory of the newest John Deere models. I tend to believe that it had more to do with my great butt, short skirts, sultry legs, and stiletto pumps than my tractor selection. At this stage…whatever works. And I was all about "workin" it to my advantage. I soon was making more money than I had ever made in my life. In small, rural Sticksville, I had become "Super Corporate Woman." I knew that Gloria Steinem and all the bra burning gals of the seventies were proud of me. Although the bra size hadn't changed much, my outward appearance, greatly enhanced by stainless steel under wire and voluminous padding, and the incredible accomplishments over the last few years earned me more than enough credits to burn it honorably as well as access to the secret handshake. I had finally made it. I had become a mover and a shaker in my own right!

Chapter Twelve

FINDING COMFORTABLE GROUND IN THE "X" RELATIONSHIP

After Bobby realized that I hadn't experienced a full blown nervous breakdown (close only counts in horseshoes) and he had completed his own course of "How to Look Like an Idiot Dating Women Young Enough to Be Your Daughter," had a few plastic surgeries (which he had me believe was a brain tumor), and bought a new expensive foreign sports car, we began to come to terms with our new relationship—or was that the un-relationship? As two virtually mature adults, we realized it was no longer about the "Cyber Lettered Woman" or "Bobby and his Barbies." It was about our children.

We spent several more months throwing intermittent zingers at each other. But all in all, it would be my tongue that would remain maimed and scarred for life as a consequence of continually biting it. Simultaneously, with my slurred speech due to the six layers of calluses on my tongue, Bobby finally ceased fire.

I think his newfound admiration came from his epiphany that being a mother was less glamorous and a great deal more work than he could have ever envisioned in his wildest hallucinogenic moments. Just the twenty-five loads of laundry alone nearly sent him into his very own nervous breakdown. He also had another revelation. The groceries, cooking meals, bill paying, housekeeping, homework and school projects, medical and dental appointments, and after school activities (just typing this makes me tired), didn't magically *just happen*! For the first time since puberty, I was quite sure that by the end of his day (somewhere around midnight or probably much later since men can't multi-task) he too was too tired for sex! I am also quite confident that after that excuse became tiresome with his "girl du jour," he too resorted to the headache story. Life does come full circle.

The biggest change in our relationship occurred when Bobby found his girl, or much to my delight, woman.

After one year of lighting candles—or was that inserting pins into my "Ken" doll—my prayers had been answered. He had found a wonderful, stable, career woman with grown children, who would prove to be a perfect second wife and stepmother to my children. Better yet, she didn't want to hang out with our daughter and borrow—or as my daughter would say, "debo"—her clothes. This was truly the second time since baptism that I knew I had been saved.

His new Mrs. and I have much in common. In fact, under different circumstances, we could have been pals. On any given soccer Saturday, the two of us can be seen conversing away while watching the children compete. I do have to be somewhat cautious because Bobby gets a wee bit tense if we talk long and laugh too loud. I am quite sure he is petrified that I may be spilling all the "Bobby Beans." Not to worry your perfectly round head, Bobby, I absolutely wouldn't dream of doing anything to jeopardize your relationship with your new wife. For the first time in four years, I do and say everything possible to convince her that she has found her true prince. This may explain my extending nose and the reoccurrence of the calluses on my tongue. Sometimes the end really does justify the means.

After watching Bobby and his new Mrs. interact, I too have had my own epiphany. In my next life I want to be the second wife. Miraculously, every bad habit Bobby had, other than scratching that conspicuous area in the morning (which I am assuming he still does), has somehow miraculously disappeared or greatly softened. I am sure I may be slightly exaggerating, yet it is pretty scary. I equate the first wife with a first car: the demo. The nicks, dings, and scrapes don't mean a thing because someday she most likely will be traded in for a new model. If traded, she will be replaced with a brand new expensive sports car that he knows must last. Consequently, his hobbies of hunting, playing poker with the boys, and being a clicker controlling couch potato have now been replaced with washing, waxing, and continually admiring his new beautiful car. Can you say Lamborghini? In my next life I am going to be Mrs. Lamborghini, not Mrs. Volkswagen.

CAUTION

Chapter Thirteen

PRE-OWNED MEN

As with pre-owned vehicles, both men and women should be able to evoke the lemon law with certain predisposed, pre-owned people. Focusing on the male character, most women would agree that many pre-owned individuals come with their very own full set of Samsonite luggage, more popularly referred to as "baggage." Some have trunks. I recently heard a great analogy on men and the dating scene at my age. Basically, men are very much like parking spots; the good ones are taken and the rest are handicapped (emotionally).

Some of these handicapped individuals have become extremely eccentric due to being alone too long. You know the type. This is the guy who puts his Star War sheets back on his king-sized bed and has a freezer full of T.V. dinners, for one. Others, who have had many long-term relationships but did not ever marry or have children, are really out there! These men never learned the rules of the toilet paper roll and where to squeeze the toothpaste, nor have they ever had to deal with a child that projectile vomits spaghetti dinner. Such an event builds strong character—or at the very least a strong stomach.

There is also the group that has been married multiple times. Their motto is "When in doubt, divorce and just keep on trying." I guess if these men live long enough, they have a minuscule chance of getting it right. They all seem to have Cybil-like personalities, most likely produced from having to adapt to multiple spouses. There is yet another group that I have labeled the "Post Traumatic Wife Syndrome" men. These guys cannot function without a wife or significant other in their lives. I equate them to chain smokers. They need to have a new cigarette lit and ready before the other one is completely burned out. They cannot be alone. The ink is barely dry on their divorce papers and they are already looking for a replacement. Delayed gratification is not in their vocabulary. These are the guys who go out with you a couple of times and, without knowing much about you, especially the not-so-wonderful stuff, fall madly in love with you regardless. After approximately one month, a serious amount of time for these guys, a Friday night date commonly entails dinner, a movie and hitting the first drive-thru church to exchange wedding vows.

The last fraternity of handicapped men is the group who has been married, commonly for a long duration, yet has quite successfully managed for a majority of their married life to get away with multiple extra-curricular interludes on the side. This species is the most dangerous of all. They are the Bill Clintons. They are both charismatic and brilliantly deceptive. These men can convince you that the "blue dress" is theirs and the stain is really Ben and Jerry's vanilla ice cream. They are the used car salesmen who possess the stealth of taking it to a whole new level. They have mastered the art of knowing exactly what women want to know, hear, and feel and use it to their full advantage. These men have street smarts gone awry.

With this summarization of the various species of midlife men, I must allow ample discussion of the man with seemingly no handicaps: the "Just Too Nice Guy." You know his type. He is the guy who does everything, as Goldilocks proclaims, "just right." Yet, to our dismay he doesn't possess the rough, "bad boy" edges we find both appealing and addicting. What's this all about? Do we need some form of abuse to make us happy?

This "Too Nice Guy" is not the guy who uses crude and vulgar street language and misuses the F word as an adjective. He is also not the guy whose eyes glaze over when a young, beautiful, overly endowed woman walks into the room, causing you to imagine this cartoon conversation bubble over his head that reads, "Boy, would I love to throw her a shot!" He also is not the guy who forgets to bring flowers and a bottle of wine to the first dinner date at your house. Most importantly, he is not the guy who comes to your house for dinner, forgets the bottle of wine and flowers, says "you're f_ _ kin' hot," throws you a shot, and *doesn't call for three days!*

But unfortunately, Mr. "Just Too Nice" is the guy, mistakenly to us and quite unfairly to him, we find boring. I guess it is true what they say: nice guys really do finish last.

LEMONADE
5¢

Chapter Fourteen

WHEN GIVEN LEMONS

My first serious (invited to at least one family holiday festivity) post divorce relationship was with Mr. "Never Been Married No Children" (NBMNC). He was wonderful to me. He wined me, dined me, bought me all sorts of beautiful and expensive trinkets, and took me everywhere. He was the consummate gentleman. However, he was extremely boring and thought my children really were Wednesday and Pugsley.

One night, during one of our initial extended family dinners, Mr. NBMNC showed his true colors. He made the lethal mistake of forcing my abundantly hormonal and quite outspoken daughter to eat bok choy, a vegetable she could neither spell nor had any desire to try. With his stern orders to sample his new addition to the quasi-family vegetable food group, my daughter instantly shifted into one of her latest multiple personalities: Regan from *The Exorcist*. Her head began to spin; she spouted a few borderline adjectives and directives and ran crying into her bedroom, slamming the door shut behind her. This episode, along with a few other such non-meetings of the minds quickly sabotaged this initial relationship. Mr. NBMNC's expensive trinkets remained, but he was out the door. I knew I should have stood my ground and served corn.

Just about the time I had purchased a new jewelry box to house all my new baubles and had permanently deleted Mr. NBMNC from my cell phone database, along came Mr. Casanova. Yes, this was the guy who had a PhD in charisma mixed with a minor in pathological lying and guiltlessness. He was the bad boy we all love to love and then hate.

Mr. Casanova was a hybrid of handsome, suave, and debonair possessed (literally) with the overly New Jersey Italian Joe Pesci character in *Goodfellas* and the charming, alluring personality of Ted Bundy less the serial killing tendency. I spent the majority of this relationship performing an exorcism and convinced I was the one who needed a good therapist and mind-altering medication.

Mr. Casanova was childlike, playful, spontaneous, and energetic—and best of all he was absolutely phenomenal in the sack. I thought I had died and gone to sex heaven. If only I had known how to get there years earlier via something equivalent to today's Map Quest, I might not have been so vulnerable. I never realized there were so many ways to achieve and experience an orgasm. I was consumed by a desire to buy a carton of cigarettes (I don't smoke) and chocolate bon bons (I don't like chocolate) and hang out in bed (on a Tempur-Pedic mattress of course) all day. I was making up for years of feeling that sex was just not all that. More than ever, I wished I was independently wealthy, or better yet, that I could be greatly compensated for doing what I'd recently learned to love best. Would this be considered prostitution? It would be monogamous and extremely high class. Yes, my new career could be an uppity, overpaid hooker.

I believe that women rediscover and redefine their sexual needs in their forties. In our twenties it's all about bonding the new marriage and eventually the need to extend the lineage. In our thirties, it's a wifely duty (remember the fine print in the marriage contract with the escape clause of an occasional headache). In our forties, the kids are grown and fairly self-reliant, leaving us less exhausted and allowing sex to be fun and more of a priority again.

Thanks in part to Mr. Casanova, I felt like a teenager again. I was getting to intimately know my body and the pleasure of being with someone in this capacity again. The significant difference was that I no longer thought anything that two consensual adults did resulted in blindness or hairy palms. For the first time in my adult life, I felt absolute sexual freedom. I knew what gave me pleasure and was forthright in voicing it. I wanted to go on the Oprah Winfrey show and jump around like a maniac and exclaim, "I love Katie!" No, that was Tom Cruise. I wanted to scream to the world, "I love sex!"

After one year of intense courtship and what we both mistakenly thought was a fair indication of our family dynamics, Mr. Casanova and I moved into a nice house in the "burbs" of Sticksville.

Chapter Fifteen

YOURS, MINE, AND NOT OURS

With all of my post divorce male relationships, the most difficult part of the initiation process was the kid thing. Whether he came into the relationship with kids or not, it always ended up a competition. He and the kids transformed into a pack of dogs, each vying for the alpha position. The whole interaction reverted into a territorial issue, peeing in corners and all. I have never seen such immaturity in all my life. And I am not just referring to the children.

Teenage children can be a handful even in the best households. Yet mix them in with their single parents and those parents' significant others and you open a whole new can of worms: bright green ones, at that. Girls continue their head spinning antics, but now have added, "You are not my Daddy/Mommy," to their repertoire of spouting declarations. Boys, on the other hand, commence their own rendition of the Oedipus complex. Once you become a single mother, your son takes over the role of the man of the house; and no dude who nonchalantly waltzes into your life is messing with his newly appointed position as Gatekeeper.

This menagerie brings out one of the major differences in men and women (other than the multi-tasking characteristic). Women do what they always do—talk too much. And men do what they always do—throw tantrums and threaten to take their toys and go home.

Mr. Casanova and I made a gallant effort to mesh two diverse households. We were a very twisted version of the Brady Bunch. Actually, we would have been better described as a fine specimen of the Bundys in our own sitcom version of *Unmarried with Children*.

This union was doomed from the start. My first indication should have been when I witnessed the movers unloading two spitting Venus DeMilo statues, a framed New England Patriots football jersey, and a holographic picture of the Last Supper from the moving van. After considerable negotiation (adeptly learned from childhood), I managed to keep them safely tucked away in the garage until I could find a home for them: the curbside on garbage pickup day.

The second bolt of lightning struck during our first quasi-family Sunday supper. I should have remembered the dinner dilemma from my last relationship. You know, a wiser woman would have opted for fast food and eating on the run. After being in the kitchen for the better part of the Sabbath (hello, what happened to resting on the seventh day?), I came to the table last, ensuring every one had everything they needed right down to a replenished wine and ice water. Before I could take my seat at the table and place my Grandma's heavily starched linen napkin in my lap, I realized my new family had almost finished their entire meal. After three more bites and a quick napkin swipe across their faces, they proceeded to excuse themselves from the table. I didn't see them again until dessert. This dining occasion served as my blatant introduction to his family traditions.

I was stunned by my new family's lack of table manners, or for that matter their total disregard for the cook. However, it was their eating habits that really got my attention. My daughter, son, and I were completely awestruck by their mastication of food. In all my years of family dining, a finely appointed table with Grandma's silver, china, linens, and all, I don't believe I have had the good fortune to be graced by the presence of a family of prehistoric raptors. My children and I got quite an eye and ear full of the many sights and sounds of food at various stages of consumption. This "chewing with their mouths closed" challenged brood sent the rest of us into sensory overload and stifled our appetites. In time we quit staring in total amazement and disgust and handled the seating arrangement in such a way as to negate any further opportunity of sitting directly across from these unsavory creatures. By this time, my kids and I had dropped five pounds. What a diet plan!

Even though meals together were not pretty and my new raptor family had some additional rough edges that were in desperate need of smoothing, the most difficult aspect of this union was managing our family squabbles. Naturally, all children bicker and fight. But the intensity and the character of an altercation of a mixed family whose personalities and life experiences are on the opposite ends of the continuum are quite surreal. Everything comes down to "this is not the way we do it at our house."

This dilemma was magnified by two entirely different parental discipline styles. I would send the children, his and mine, to their rooms until they cooled off; or if the incident was serious enough, I would ground them and/or take something of great importance away for a period of time. With this plan of attack, I would be instantly met with his children's declarations of "You are not my mother. I want to go home." Mr. Casanova, on the other hand, would begin screaming loud enough for the entire county to hear, spewing long tirades of obscenities. With this, my children would run for cover and have long discussions behind closed bedroom doors on the merits of washing his mouth out with soap for such profanities. They too would spout off that he was not their father, declaring their hope that this family would pack their bags and move back into their own house as quickly as they had come.

The culminating blow to this relationship had nothing to do with the children or our dichotomous life or parenting styles. Unfortunately, like the real Casanova, my Mr. Casanova also had a propensity for women—multiple women simultaneously. He made the Julio Iglesias song "For All the Girls I've Loved Before" sound like a celibacy ballad. He had his own rendition entitled "For All the Girls I've Loved Before, During and After," and he gave new meaning to the catch phrase "share the love." Mr. Casanova's lust for women was equally matched by his mastered art of deception. He could weave a tale better than most *New York Times* best- selling authors. He had me blindly convinced I was the only one. Yeah, maybe on my *block*!

The most pathetic part of this story is that Mr. Casanova had very little remorse. He even had the audacity to call me the day after I caught him and offered to make amends by cooking me dinner: spaghetti and meatballs, of course. Even more ironic, or should I say humorous, was that his profile on an Internet dating site read, "I am a one-woman kind of guy." Isn't that false advertisement? Needless to say, I sent Mr. Casanova packing!

The most invaluable lesson I learned from this liaison is never to bring a man into my household in that fashion again until my children are successfully moved out of the house, or he has been neutered and I am heavily medicated.

Chapter Sixteen

THE CONTINUED IMPORTANCE OF GAL PALS

During our teenage years, our girlfriends take precedence over all of our other relationships. We would spend many a Saturday night sleepover trying on each other's clothes, styling each other's hair, painting each other's nails with the newest fluorescent color, pondering our futures, and devising a master plan to capture the hottest guy in school. We divulged secrets and discussed topics we would rather die than tell our seemingly "dinosaur" parents. After all, wasn't the whole sex thing, like them, extinct by their age?

We would hole ourselves up in our locked bedrooms with makeshift milk cartons containing inconspicuous samplings of alcohol we'd stolen from our parents' liquor cabinets. It tasted horrific but produced the effect we were going after: a good buzz. Feeling slightly tipsy, we would roll around the bedroom floor giggling and recalling our latest anecdotes concerning the opposite sex. Most of our discussions revolved around the age-old penis size debate and if certain medieval practices really thwarted pregnancy.

Once again, as a forty-eight year old single woman, my single girlfriends have shifted back into playing a very significant role in my life. We still do sleepovers. However, now, our pajama parties consist of a gourmet meal served with a bottle of Sterling Merlot, hanging out in the hot tub, hiring in a gorgeous male masseur, pondering our next getaway together, and working on each other's online dating profiles in an attempt to capture the hottest available guy within a fifty-mile radius of Sticksville. I have come to the conclusion that the perfect man just may be Mr. Potato Head. He is cute, tan, and understands the importance of accessorizing. If he steps out of line, you can rearrange his face.

Feeling quite tipsy after polishing off three bottles of exceptional wine, we once again find ourselves giggling on the living room floor, consumed with schoolgirl chatter about the opposite sex. Only now, our conversations center around Viagra, Cialis, and the prospect of being with the man whose erection lasts more than four hours. There are two schools of thought on this subject from my gal pals. The first is the hope that it lasts for more then four minutes...but if, God forbid it lasts more than four hours, don't call the doctor. Just shoot the bastard in self-defense! The second school of thought is that if his erection lasts more than four hours, don't talk to anyone! Bolt the doors, shut the shades, let the phones go to voicemail, turn on Lionel Ritchie's eighties hit song "Endless Love," and completely succumb to the ecstasy. If, after the four-hour benchmark, he begins to turn blue, then and only then, call the doctor!

Even as a single woman in midlife with all the confidence in the world, I still feel like a teenager in the dating scene again. I feel many of the insecurities and inadequacies I felt at sixteen years old. I begin this self-talk nonsense. "Do I look my age? Am I still sexy? Have I been successful camouflaging that new wrinkle? Should I have my breasts enlarged or at least put back where they used to be?" After meeting a guy with potential (about 1 in 10,000), I still feel the high school girl pangs of "Does he like me? Should I let him kiss me? Will he call?" Then, if all goes well and I begin the dating ritual, I am posed with the million-dollar question: "How long should I wait before going to bed with him?" This debate still gives me the willies. Is it still fashionable to wait thirty days? Or, due to our new instant world, is it some derivative thereof? As a new millennium woman, I beg the question, "Where do men draw the line between slut and spontaneous?" Are promiscuous women my age still sluts or just sexually explicit? My gal pals and I have spent many a wine induced night contemplating such distinctions.

We still continue to debate the answer to the age-old question concerning the opposite sex: "What on earth are they thinking?" Quite humorously, thirty some years later, we are still in total agreement. We don't have a frickin' clue.

Not all of our conversations are so immature and lighthearted. On occasion, we discuss more serious "new millennium dating world" issues. Our most pressing concern today is life-threatening sexually transmitted diseases. Yesterday's worries of pregnancy or an infection that once could be cleared up by a strong antibiotic have been replaced by a well-warranted fear of dying. When we have established our personally accepted time limit with someone and are ready to embark into the sexual frontier, how do we broach this delicate subject? We could be completely forthright and ask, "Do you have any STDs? Have you engaged in risky sexual behavior?" Yeah right! This is as preposterous as the security personnel at the airport asking, "Are you carrying any weapons or bombs? Have you ever engaged in any terrorist activity?" If the answers to any of these questions are truly yes, are we unrealistic enough to believe that this person will own up to it? I can see it now. After thirty dates (my personal benchmark), as I am teetering on the brink of the "act," my newest love interest breathlessly declares he is a member of Palestinian National Liberation Movement, is carrying a bomb, and has tested positive for AIDS.

As I end this discussion, I would be remiss if I didn't pose one other age-old query: "Can men and women really be friends?" Can we girls have guy pals?

No, I am not referring to the Y Generation's "friends with benefits" type of opposite sex relationship. I am talking about the true benefits of having a guy pal in your life. Someone that you can just hang out with, that is there for you, and that you can talk to for hours concerning your past, present, and future, including the pathetic tales of your traditional relationships with members of his male fraternity. The best part of this guy pal relationship is being able to engage in all this without benefit of makeup, a good hair day, or a need to come up with excuses for not wanting to have sex with him!

Is this possible or just one estrogen-charged idealist's fantasy? Not only do I believe it to be possible, I am blessed with one of the best guy pals in the world or at least the far-reaching corners of Sticksville.

My best guy buddy is Mr. Mustard (affectionately called this because he drives a yellow pickup truck). Mr. Mustard can negotiate with the best of me, is equally quick-witted, and actually gets my off-the-wall thought process. He astutely and aptly engages in my harmless bantering. He adores and even thrives on my borderline sarcasm. My male bud can keep me on my toes and as sharp as a No. 2 pencil in elementary school. Best of all, this guy has a strong feminine side (a real oxymoron) and is not dissuaded by my endless efforts to impede his sexual innuendos. His testosterone and male ego will not allow him to stop trying, but our endearing friendship keeps the non-sexual part of our relationship in line. It really is the best of both worlds. I can get his take on women without ever having to take my clothes off!

Chapter Seventeen

THE NEW FAIRY TALE AGED TO PERFECTION

Quite unlike my dysfunctional post parental divorce upbringing, both of my children have remained, in my opinion, fairly unscathed. During the breakup of our family, both Bobby and I were in total (more me than him) agreement that our children would benefit greatly from family therapy. Bobby's fear that they might turn out like me most likely encouraged him to take this course of action. Unlike our marriage counseling, he actually showed up more than once. I never did get the opportunity to tell my side of the story but, more importantly, our children did. Our commitment to their mental health was foremost in both of our minds and actions. This healthy and unselfish attitude is the reason they are so well adjusted. Above and beyond anything that ever transpired between Bobby and me, they are loved by both of us more than anything in this world. They are the most incredible by-products of our twenty-three year union.

Bobby, his Mrs., and I have a strong connection and play integral roles in our children's upbringing. We have a family powwow at least once a month just to make sure our two households are in synch and on track. We, as a united trio of parents, make it known to the kids that nothing gets by us and that there is zero tolerance for playing us against each other. Our expectations for them remain the same no matter the household. We, as parents, are on the same playing field. Our main objective is to get the job done and get it done right. Once that has been accomplished, we will liquidate everything and enter the witness protection program.

As for me, once in a while, usually every third waxing moon, I feel the need to have my very own pity party. I have a few glasses of wine, turn on emotionally moving music usually —Andrea Bocelli or Josh Groban—and shed a few tears for all the woulda, coulda, shouldas. These one-person parties don't last long. I usually soak in a nice bubble bath, apply a refining face masque, put on my favorite nubby flannel jammies, hop into my king-sized bed for one, have a good talk with the man upstairs, and fall asleep anticipating a brand new day. This ritual usually does not let me down!

I still contemplate the breast augmentation debate. At one point, I even began saving my spare change for a consultation. I was not very successful. Just about the time I had a few dollars saved, the kids emptied the Mason jar for their milk money. I have settled for the curve appeal (or would that be curb appeal) offered by the industrial line of Frederick's of Hollywood.

As for men, I am still awaiting the second coming of Prince Charming. I don't have quite the once-overly zealous anticipation, but nonetheless there is some hopeful "before I leave the planet" expectation. The good news is that I still have my ball gown. The bad news is it's got some wrinkles. More importantly, now that I am queen, wouldn't I outrank him? For many men, this could be a problem. Maybe I am destined to occupy the throne alone.

I have remained so shell-shocked from my episode with Mr. Casanova that I haven't really allowed myself to be out there or even consider the possibility of a new relationship. Additionally, with my demanding career and the ever-busy schedules of my children, I really have not had a window of opportunity to pursue anything too serious. Besides, I have come to truly enjoy my own company. It affords great one-sided conversation: mine. My aging, still virginal aunt coined a wonderful term for what I am becoming at this stage in my dating life: "man-orexic." She just may be right!

At one bleak and desperate singlehood moment, I found myself perusing two popular Internet dating sites. Once again, I came across Mr. Casanova's profile. His continued pile of horse poop, including still being a "one woman kind of man" has tarnished my image of such sites and the accuracy of their members. One guy claimed in his profile that he was not a serial dater. Does that mean he prefers eggs in the morning?

Several months ago, on a plane ride home from a national John Deere franchise owner convention, I came across an advertisement in the in-flight magazine for a dating service for extremely busy professionals like me called "It's Just a Snack." I presumed this was a spin-off of the less busy professionals' dating service, "It's Just Lunch." The "It's Just a Snack" advertisement contained rave reviews from other busy professional women who had met good prospects through this service (only women my age refer to available, noteworthy men as "good prospects").

As I drove home from the airport that day, I began my self-questioning ritual again. Did I really need to engage such a service or was I just in desperate need of a night out on the town with my gal pals, or perhaps a good romantic chick flick or a mindless romance novel?

The following week, I spent some time investigating this service. After doing a little homework and making some inquiries, I came to the conclusion that my money and time could be better spent taking a much-needed long weekend at my favorite spa.

Every so often, I revisit the dating service possibility. I remain on the fence—or more apropos, out to lunch. But I have come to a revelation concerning the dating/mating dance; whether we are sixteen or sixty, the man enters into this ritual contemplating the moment, while the woman contemplates her future. The first time new couples wake up together, the man checks his equipment (which fortunately or unfortunately, depending on each woman's preferences, is wide awake and standing at attention) and wonders if there will be morning sex, while the woman on the other hand, bolts to the bathroom to pee (our post-childbearing curse), wonders whether he will join her in brushing the mittens off his teeth, and begins envisioning the color selections of their new house. If I ever get a second go-round at all of this, I have decided I am playing the role of Samantha in *Sex and the City* (or in Sticksville, Sex and the Country). I am quite confident that her laissez-faire attitude is less painful or at the very least less guilt ridden.

My sexual satisfaction remains thanks to my battery powered French lover Pierre. My search for a good housewife continues. By the time I put in a full day at the tractor dealership, drop off and pick up the kids from soccer practice and piano lessons, make a quick pit stop for grocery essentials, cook dinner, assist with algebra homework, and tuck the kids into bed (even though they are teenagers, I still find pleasure in this), I fall into bed, read three or four pages of my latest book, and plunge into a coma.

One night after two glasses of Merlot, my son lovingly offered to rub my feet. He asked me to position myself comfortably on the couch, lay my head on the pillow, and close my eyes. I woke up three days later! I should have given a tad more consideration to flying solo, coupled with the demands of raising two teenage children at forty-eight years old! Had the batteries gone dead in my calculator when I began my stroll down Infertility Lane? More aptly, I believe it was my brain that may have gone dead. For the "gazillionth" time, "What in the H-E-double toothpicks was I thinking?" Let's be depressingly realistic. I could be a grandmother! No, at my age, I should be a grandmother. I'm not too fond of the title but at least I could spoil the little cherubs rotten, send them home to their parents and take a nap. I am too old for this nonsense! I find it increasingly difficult to retain my youthful appearance raising two puberty plagued offspring. Yeah, the almost fifty may be the new forty if you are not teaching your sixteen year old daughter to drive a standard five speed in the center of Sticksville's busiest intersection. (The presence of livestock lends new perspective to defensive driving.) It's just wrong. At my age, it's not a threat; I really could have a heart attack!

Most of the time, even with a demanding career, I am confident in my continued reign of "Best Single Mom of the Year." Yet, every so often, as much as I hate to admit it, my title is threatened.

One day during the peak season at the store, I received a phone call from my son's school. It was the school nurse. She said my son was complaining of a stomachache and wanted me to pick him up and take him home. I explained to her that he tends to be a bit of a hypochondriac and will come up with any excuse to get an occasional reprieve from school. I politely indicated that unless he had a temperature and was close to dying, she was not to bother me again with his nonsense.

Approximately one hour went by and the school nurse called again. This time I was not so nice. I sternly reminded her that unless his supposed illness was life threatening, I could not afford to take time away from my extremely busy workday to come and get him. I requested that she allow him to rest for a bit and then send his butt back to class. She sheepishly agreed and hung up the phone.

Another forty-five minutes went by when my office manager interrupted my conference call with the southern territory John Deere sales rep and indicated that my son's school was on the other line. I put the rep on hold and angrily picked up the other line and said, "Now what?" Only this time, it was not the school nurse but the principal of my son's school, and now she was the one who was stern and impolite. As she explained the situation with my son, I began to slink down in my wonderfully comfortable high-backed, "mover and shaker" leather chair. It seems that not only was my son not fabricating a tale of sickness, he had just vomited all over her and her very "principal" looking desk. As I sped over to the school like a Mario Andretti wannabe, I entertained thoughts of transferring him to another school to keep both my ego and Mother of the Year title intact. To this day, I still hang my head in shame and maintain minimal eye contact with the school office personnel. I just know if these women had their way, they would strip me of my crown!

Even though Bobby and I have been divorced for several years, I have remained actively involved in running his household, at least when the children are with him. I guess you could say we now have a long distance relationship. It's astounding! Every time our children have school projects, medical appointments, or any outside or after school activities, I have to fax him, e-mail him, and call him; and then I call his new wife to remind her to remind him that I have reminded him. The added phone calls and paperwork alone wear me out. I am no longer his wife. I am his secretary! I have become his human palm pilot, appointment alarms and all. The only difference is that now I am absolved from having to perform wifely duties. Some days, I think I just should have remained his wife…*not*!

The Awakening

The Continuation

FULL CIRCLE

I am lounging in REM sleep. Oh, what a dream! To my relief, I vaguely hear a disturbance echoing in my ears. This welcome noise becomes louder and louder with each passing second, forcing me out of this seemingly endless night of reflection. In an instant, totally at my will, reality replaces REM. It is six a.m., and that sound is my alarm clock awakening me to the rest of my life. Reality is wonderful!

As I begin to clear the cobwebs from my brain, wipe the "sleepies" from my eyes, and let out a lengthy sigh, a beaming smile envelops my face. Waking up to yet another forty-something-year-old day does not suck. Today and every day hereafter begins the rest of my life. My entire life, the good, the bad, and the ugly, has brought me to who and where I am today, with the people I cherish. If one part of this puzzle was missing, the picture, my life's picture, would be incomplete. The road I took, sometimes smooth, oftentimes laced with potholes, has brought me to me: Abagal Smart, a forty-eight year old single mom.

Remarkably, my equation to Dorothy in The Wizard of Oz remains appropriate. I, like Dorothy, believed that my life would be so much better "somewhere over the rainbow." However, also like Dorothy, after one very long night's dream, I too have come to realize that there really is "no place like home"!

At this stage of my life, I have pretty much come full circle. I am now the queen of my own castle. My kingdom is still Sticksville. But this rural area, which at times seems like a death sentence or at least a very strict penance, has afforded a wonderful, safe, and secure life for my children.

My daughter is now a junior in high school and very much her own woman. She is confident and has street smarts well beyond her years—her father's daughter. She is a bright young woman who believes everything in life is her way or the highway and has the somewhat cocky attitude that matches this thought process. She is a leader, stands her ground, and fights for her beliefs. At this stage of her life, some of these include that girls should have at least one Coach Bag, be allowed to have their belly buttons pierced on their sixteenth birthdays, and have a hair shade that continually coordinates with her name brand outfits. (I am only slightly exaggerating.)

Thanks to an extremely fortunate lifestyle with two very successful parents, my daughter is cultured, well traveled, and fairly sophisticated. Her idea of camping is microwaving popcorn at the Holiday Inn. She has become my partner in crime in my frequent visits to the Big Apple; quite like me and Eva, she too longs for Park Avenue. However, I am proud to say she remains humble. Her friends represent a melting pot of all walks of life and family dynamics, and she is always ready and willing to support the underdog and assist the less fortunate.

The most important lesson I hope she has learned from me is that she must be a woman who can stand on her own and preferably not next to a John Deere tractor. I continually instill the analogy that she is the cake, and whoever ends up being the man in her life is the icing. This wonderfully sweet stuff should complement the cake but never overpower it.

My son is in middle school and has become quite the little man of my household. He is a sweet, sensitive, loving young man, who thinks his mother doesn't need anyone in her life as long as she has him. He continually threatens that he has no intentions of ever moving out and that, should he ever entertain marriage, he will set up his new family camp with me. This evokes an image of a sixties commune of the very worst kind. At this moment, I am keeping my future intentions completely under wraps. I plan to sell the house when my son is eighteen, buy a Prevost bus, and hit the open road with no forwarding address.

This young man is truly my son. Quite like me, he has the gift of humor meshed with a very creative, busy, and preoccupied mind. We are continually in competition to be the last one ready to go anywhere and the first one to find the car keys. We are members of an extremely elite group who, upon returning home from grocery shopping, open all the jars labeled "refrigerate after opening" and then quite appropriately stick them in the fridge. *Hello*.... is there problem with this? We both dance to a beat very few people hear. This totally frustrates his somewhat conservative and extremely organized sister. But what makes us, us, is that we are not bothered by this one tiny bit.

All in all, I am very content and secure with who I am and what I have become. It only took forty-eight years! I have managed, with an adequate supply of crazy glue, to stay intact and fairly mentally healthy. A smidgen of "dys-functionality" keeps me interesting. This is not to say that I won't momentarily veer off the road again. Life has a way of throwing obstacles at you. But now, I have the skills and confidence to circumvent some of these pitfalls, get right back on my bicycle and the road of life.

Looking back one last time before closing this chapter of my life, I know better than ever before that I am genuinely the product of where I have been, whom I have met, and what I have done. **Footnote # 9:** I am very pleased with the woman and the journey…**and yes, I am still pedaling as fast as I can, destination unknown!**

www.ingramcontent.com/pod-product-compliance
Lightning Source LLC
LaVergne TN
LVHW012333100826
845148LV00017B/2131

* 9 7 8 1 5 9 9 3 2 0 6 9 4 *